Oklahoma Centennial
Title 1
FY: 11/12   12/13   13/14
SIG   ARRA

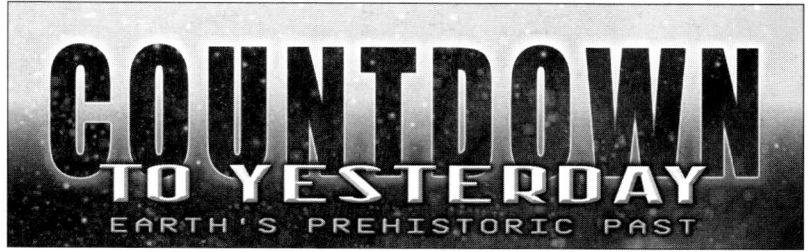

by
Ellen Hopkins

Perfection Learning®

Cover illustration and design: Michael A. Aspengren
Inside layout and design: Michelle J. Glass

About the Author

Ellen Hopkins lives with her family, four dogs, two cats, and three tanks of fish near Carson City, Nevada. A California native, Ellen moved to the Sierra Nevada to ski. While writing for a Lake Tahoe newspaper, she discovered many exciting things and fascinating people.

Illustration: Larry Nolte p. 7; Michael Aspengren p. 61

Image credits: ©CORBIS pp. 10, 34, 60; National Geographic p. 64

ArtToday (some images copyright www.arttoday.com) pp. 11, 21, 22, 28 (bottom), 31, 33, 36 (bottom), 39, 46, 50, 53, 59; Corel Professional Photos pp. 4, 5, (top), all small dinosaurs at the beginning of each chapter, 14 (background), 16–17, 23, 24, 25, 28 (top), 29, 30, 36 (top), 37, 40, 41, 42, 43, 44, 47, 54, 56–57, 67; Hemera Studio.com p. 6; Photodisc pp. 9, 15, 27; U.S. Geological Survey p. 12; photo courtesy of Richard Hallock p. 5 (bottom)

Text © 2002 by Perfection Learning® Corporation.
All rights reserved. No part of this book may be reproduced, stored in a retrieval system, or transmitted in any form or by any means, electronic, mechanical, photocopying, recording, or otherwise, without prior permission of the publisher.
Printed in the United States of America. For information, contact Perfection Learning® Corporation, 1000 North Second Avenue, P.O. Box 500, Logan, Iowa 51546-0500.
Tel: 1-800-831-4190 • Fax: 1-800-543-2745
Paperback ISBN 0-7891-5499-4
Cover Craft® ISBN 0-7569-0249-5

TABLE OF CONTENTS

Introduction 4

Chapter 1 Minus Five Billion 5

Chapter 2 Reading Rocks 9

Chapter 3 Supercontinents. 16

Chapter 4 The Living Sea 22

Chapter 5 Sculpted by Fire and Water 30

Chapter 6 Dino Detectives. 34

Chapter 7 T-Rexes in Texas 40

Chapter 8 Dinosaur Doomsday. 49

Chapter 9 Mammals Take Over. 53

Chapter 10 The Very First Americans 59

A Final Word 67

Glossary 68

Index. 71

INTRODUCTION

Did you ever wonder where the earth came from? When did it form? How long did it take? Was it always the same? What did this "Blue Planet" look like, say, 100 million years ago? Were there continents? Did they look like they do today? Did North and South America even exist?

These questions have led to serious **debate** for more than 1,000 years. Many people have different theories and beliefs about the earth's formation. Let's explore just one of the more popular scientific theories.

Our universe began as a whirling ring of gas and matter. Some little speck of that matter became Earth. It didn't happen overnight. It took millions of years for that little speck to join others, grow big and hot, and then cool and shrink. And after all that, you wouldn't have recognized the place.

One hundred million years ago, the earth looked very different. Imagine ferns in Antarctica and rain forests in Greenland. Think of monster crocodiles stalking Alaska. And don't forget dinosaurs. On land, in the sea, and in the air, giant reptiles ruled! T-Rexes in Texas? You bet, but that's only the beginning.

Hop into my time machine. Hit rewind. Set the date to minus 5 billion years. Get ready for a rocket ride into the earth's **prehistoric** past. Better fasten your seat belt!

chapter 1
Minus Five Billion

Traveling backward through time is so weird! Looking down at the earth from the time machine, we watch buildings and highways disappear. Mountains crumble into the seas as our planet folds into itself. The earth has become a spinning ball of fire.

Now it's shrinking. Smaller, smaller. Finally, it bursts apart, shooting tiny particles into space. These are the teensiest bits of matter. They are much too small to have **gravity**. And without the pull of gravity, they move at warp speed.

Wait. Slow down. Put this time machine in neutral. How far back have we gone? Our instruments read minus 5 billion. It's 5 billion years ago!

The time machine starts spinning. It's a speck, one of billions, whirling within a giant disk of gas and dust. All of these specks of matter are whirling, twirling, and bumping one another. They create heat energy. Most of the energy rushes toward the center of the spinning disk. This is where gravity begins. And that's where we find the sun.

But here at the outer edge of the disk, it's very cold. Freezing, in fact.

The specks join and grow by sweeping up other specks that come near. Gravity goes to work, sucking those little pieces closer together. That creates heat energy and makes them hot. But they never get as big and hot as the sun. They don't keep burning like the sun. Instead, they slowly cool and become planets.

Look. See that planet. The third one from the sun? "Planet Orange" is Earth. It won't be the "Blue Planet" for a while.

Water hasn't formed yet! Right now, Earth is a flaming **sphere** of melted metals and elements. Elements are simple substances like sulfur or hydrogen. They don't break down any smaller.

Check it out. The earth is shrinking. That means it's cooling. As it does, heavy metals like nickel and iron fall into the

6

middle of the fiery ball. They harden and become the earth's **core**. The center of the core is solid. But the outer part is liquid and ultra hot. The temperature there is 12,000°F!

All of that heat pulses outward, traveling in circles. It melts rock as it swirls. This mushy layer of rock is the mantle. It's about 1,800 feet thick. The mantle rises and cools. Near the surface, it hardens to form the earth's crust. The crust is our planet's shell.

Our time machine moves forward to 4 billion years ago. The cooling earth is not a friendly place. Its burning surface pitches and rolls. It looks like it's breathing. Watch out for that **exhale**! Poisonous gases, such methane and ammonia, wheeze from cracks in the crust. Volcanoes spit ash and **magma**.

Have you ever seen so much steam? The shrinking planet squeezes water **vapor** up into the toxic **atmosphere**. Clouds form. They build and swell with water vapor. Over time, dark clouds cover the earth's entire surface.

Finally, it rains. Not a sprinkle. Not a downpour. We're talking monster rains that **drench** the earth. The rain hits the hot rocks below. *Hiss!* The moisture turns to steam and rises up to become rain again.

It pours for thousands of years. Rivers of rain sweep down mountainsides. Gullies and valleys fill to the brim, becoming lakes and seas. In time, water covers 71 percent of our planet. No other planet in our solar system comes close to being this wet.

Overhead, the atmosphere is changing. At first, it's mostly hydrogen and helium. But those gases are light. They escape into space. Meanwhile, volcanoes burp other gases and vapors. Gravity holds some of them, mainly the carbon dioxide and nitrogen. This atmosphere is better. But it still has no oxygen.

Before oxygen, the earth had no ozone layer. This is an oxygen-rich layer of our atmosphere. It protects the earth from the sun's harmful radiation. Before oxygen, the sun blasted our planet with radiation. Good thing we're moving on.

> Radiation is intense rays of heat energy. In small doses, radiation can be useful. But high levels can cause everything from sunburn to cancer.
>
> Few life-forms could survive a place with no oxygen and way too much radiation. But somehow, some way, some life-forms did.
>
> Some scientists have found evidence of life before oxygen or ozone. They say life on Earth began 3 billion years ago.

chapter

Reading Rocks

Wait a minute, you say. Put this time machine in neutral again. How does anyone know the earth is 5 billion years old? How can anyone know when life began?

The answer is they "read" rocks and the fossils they contain. Fossils are the remains of ancient animals and plants surrounded by rock. Usually, the remains were things that wouldn't rot, such as shells, bones, hardwood, or teeth.

Trace fossils are footprints, trails, or burrows preserved in rock. Scientists value these because they show how prehistoric animals lived.

Microfossils are so small that it takes a microscope to see them. Some were spores or grains of **pollen**. Others resemble modern algae, fungi, and lichens. Still others are very tiny, hollow tubes. These were bacteria that looked like living threads.

Not so long ago, people had no clue what fossils were. Or how old the earth was. In the 1750s, the Industrial Revolution began. Miners and engineers built roads and canals. Sometimes they had to tunnel through hillsides. They noticed layers formed by different kinds of rock. Those layers told incredible stories.

One interested reader was James Hutton, a Scottish farmer, doctor, and chemist. As he farmed, Hutton became fascinated with soil and rock. In the 1780s, he made two very important discoveries.

James Hutton

At Glen Tilt, Scotland, Hutton found layers of limestone, shale, and granite. He saw that limestone and shale began as soft **sediments**. They settled on the bottom of the sea. Over time, they **compressed** under the weight of more sediments that settled on top of them. Finally, the soft sediments turned to stone.

Then the sea **receded**. Wind and weather chewed at the exposed rock. This **erosion** crumbled the top layer, turning it into soil. Rain washed the soil into rivers and streams. They carried the soil particles back to the sea.

These sediments settled and compacted. They turned into rock. The cycle began again. Layer upon layer of sediments built up. This created rocks like limestone, sandstone, and shale.

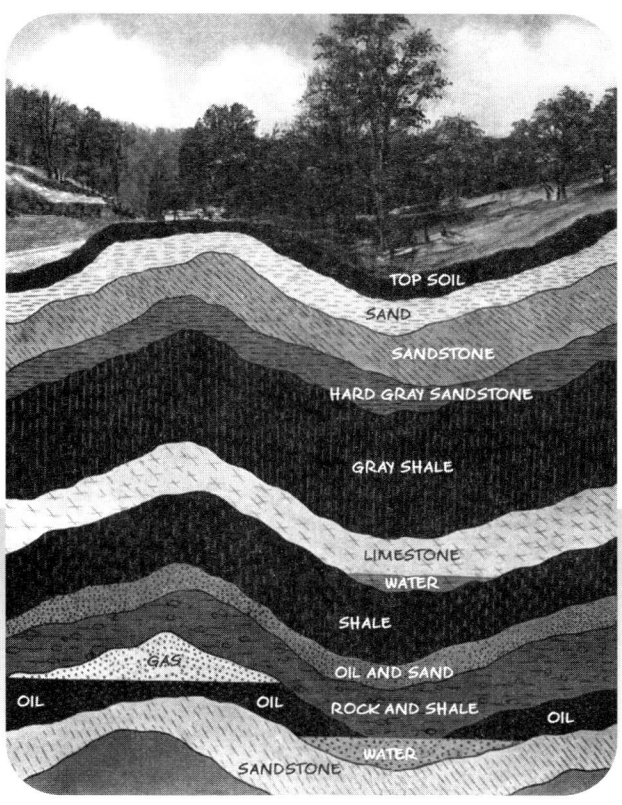

At Glen Tilt, veins of granite thrust up through the sedimentary layers. Hutton figured granite was once molten rock. It had gushed from the earth's interior, cooled, and hardened. This type of rock is called *igneous rock*.

Hutton decided both heat and water played important roles in building the planet. And so did time. His second discovery convinced him of that.

This is how it looks:

EON	ERA	PERIOD	EPOCH
	Precambrian Time 4.6 billion years ago		
Archaean			
	Precambrian Time 2.4 billion years ago		
Proterozoic			
	570 million years ago		
Phanerozoic	Paleozoic	Cambrian	
		Ordovician	
		Silurian	
		Devonian	
		Carboniferous	
		Permian	
	230 million years ago		
	Mesozoic	Triassic	
		Jurassic	
		Cretaceous	
	70 million years		
	Cenozoic	Teritiary	Paleocene
			Eocene
			Oligocene
			Miocene
			Pliocene
		3 million years ago	
		Quaternary	Pleistocene
			Holocene (recent)

The first two eons, together called Precambrian (pree–KAM–bree–un) time, make up 90 percent of our planet's history. Microfossils first appeared 3 billion years ago, in the Archaean (ar–KEE–un) eon. **Marine** fossils popped up 400 million years back, in Cambrian time.

Today, animals and plants vary from continent to continent. But fossils tell us this wasn't always so. The record is very clear. It's right here—written in rock.

chapter 3

Supercontinents

Okay, we're at 3 billion years ago—halfway through the Archaean eon. How can any life survive? The earth has cooled on the outside. But inside, it's still megahot. Hotter than it will be in the year 2005. By then, radioactive decay will have released a lot of heat.

Hot mantle rises from the earth's core. It cools as it nears the surface. Then the cooler mantle sinks. This constant cycle is called *convection*. Convection keeps the melted rock churning like cement in a cement mixer.

Some molten rock creeps up into the seafloor. It hardens as it cools, forming **oceanic** crust. This undersea crust is only about $4\frac{1}{2}$ miles thick. That's a pretty thin skin to hold all that heat inside.

Sometimes magma explodes right through the crust. Underwater volcanoes erupt. They make islands of pillow-shaped lava. Some islands grow, inch by inch, layer by layer.

Weather chews the top layer of rock into soil. Streams and rivers carry it back to the sea. The sediments collect at the islands' edges, building underwater shelves. On shore, pools of mud simmer and bubble.

Right now, there is only one ocean. It's a single body of water. Seawater leaks through cracks in the oceanic crust. The water superheats then gushes toward the surface. These undersea geysers carry minerals and gases. Some shoot all the way to the surface. Others build underwater structures called *chimneys*.

Scientists believe life on earth began in these undersea hot springs. The first bacteria "ate" poisonous chemicals bubbling up through the crust. This process is called *chemosynthesis* (kee–moh–SIN–thuh–sus).

Algae appear in hot springs on the surface of the earth. These algae build strange mounds called *stromatolites* (stroh–MAT–uh–lites). Now the sun goes to work in a magic process called *photosynthesis* (foh–toh–SIN–thuh–sus). It helps the algae soak up carbon dioxide and release oxygen. The atmosphere changes yet again as oxygen replaces carbon dioxide.

And how do we know all this? You guessed it! By reading rocks. The oldest found so far are the Acasta gneisses (NICE–suhs) in northwest Canada. Gneiss is deformed granite. The gneiss at Acasta has been dated at 4 billion years old.

Other important Archaean rocks are greenstones, granites, and komatiites (KOH–mah–tyts). Greenstones are igneous rocks that formed beneath the ocean. Later, they changed. Igneous or sedimentary rocks that have changed are called *metamorphic*.

Copper, zinc, and nickel are all found in Archaean greenstones. Gold is found in Archaean granites. Over half the gold that has been taken from the earth comes from the Witwatersrand sediments. These South African rocks are 2.9 billion years old.

> Witwatersrand means "white water ridge" in Afrik. This area, often referred to as the Rand, forms a **watershed** between the Vaal and Olifants Rivers in South Africa. The Rand is one of the world's richest gold-mining regions.

Komatiite is a type of lava that needs extremely high temperatures to form. The presence of these rocks means that the earth is much hotter in the Archaean eon than in the time we left home.

Because of the greater heat during this period, convection is also greater. The mantle churns faster and hotter. Riding above that molten rock, the earth's crust also moves. In some places, it cracks completely. The crust breaks into pieces called *plates*.

Like the mantle, the earth's plates are in constant motion. Sometimes they bump one another, and *baboom!* Earthquake! If they move apart, new crust bubbles up to fill in the cracks. This is known as *seafloor spreading*.

Sometimes one plate slides under another. This is called *subduction*. Where the upper plate is lifted, mountains grow. The lower plate's edge is forced down into the mantle. That creates deep undersea trenches. In the mantle, the subducted crust remelts. Then it cools and hardens again. The earth's crust constantly recycles itself!

Subduction also helps build continents. Continents grow at the plates' edges when crust is scraped off during subduction. As a result, continental crust is much thicker than the undersea type.

Were there continents in the Archaean eon? Scientists say yes. But they have only found small pieces of Archaean continental crust. The earliest continents were small. They probably sank back into the mantle during subduction.

All seven of today's continents are light and **buoyant**. To find where they came from, let's fast forward several million years.

Stop the time machine at 500 million years ago — Cambrian period. Convection and subduction have built continents. Several sit near the **equator**. One day, they will become North America, Europe, and Asia.

Below them sits Gondwana (gone–DWAH–nuh). This continent will one day become South America, Australia, Antarctica, and Africa. A narrow waterway, the Tethys (TEE–thus) Sea, separates Gondwana from the others.

Right now, India is located to the east of Gondwana.

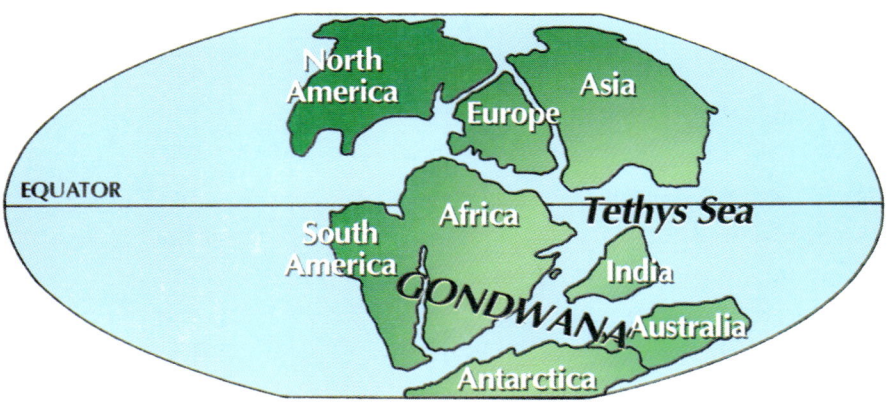

The earth's crust is always moving. Over the next 100 million years, Gondwana will drift down over the south pole. Africa will be covered with thick sheets of ice called *glaciers*. Evidence of this glacial past have been found in the Sahara Desert.

Are the earth's plates still moving today? You bet! As you read this, the ground beneath you creeps westward. It's not going very fast, of course. The North American plate moves about one inch every year. As it does, it bumps the Pacific plate. This causes earthquakes. The Pacific coast, from Alaska to Mexico, often has terrible earthquakes.

Across the Atlantic, Europe and Africa are moving together. The eastern part of Africa is separating from the rest of the continent. Where it's tearing, a **rift valley** has opened.

Later during the Permian (purr–ME–un) period, everything will shift again. Gondwana and the smaller continents will merge into a giant continent called Pangaea (pan–JEE–uh). It will straddle the equator. Everything there is warm, wet, and lush. Plants and animals spread throughout Pangaea. There are no oceans to stop them. So they can move freely between Asia and Antarctica.

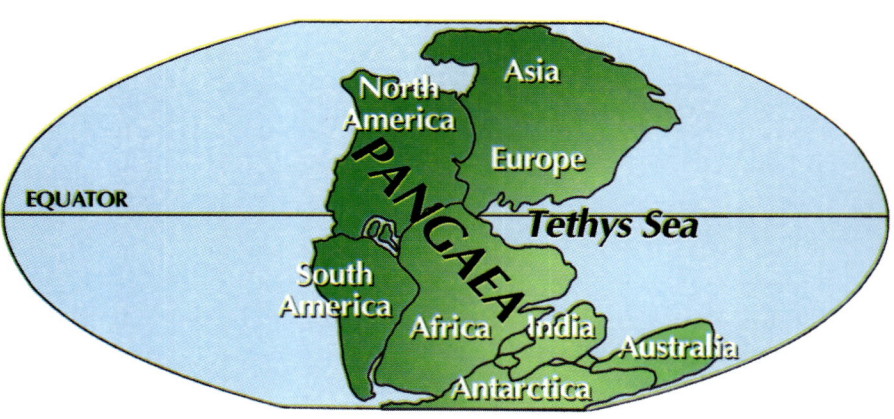

This freedom of movement explains how different continents today contain the same fossil layers. Later,

Pangaea will break apart. It won't take long, really—only 50 or 60 million years. Continental drift will move the fragments away from one another. Then these pieces will look more like today's continents.

If this seems unbelievable, study a world map. Notice how the continents look like they could fit together? Work that jigsaw puzzle; you'll get Pangaea.

> The idea of continental drift isn't new. Englishman Sir Francis Bacon mentioned the jigsaw idea in 1620. But the first to really investigate it was German meteorologist Alfred Wegener. In the early 1900s, Wegener noticed how the coastlines of South America and Africa seemed to fit together. He saw how mountain ranges on two sides of the Atlantic looked like they were once one. But what really convinced him was fossil evidence.
>
> Fossils of the same primitive fern had been found in Africa, Brazil, India, Australia, and even Antarctica. Wegener believed that meant they had all once been joined. In 1915, the world was skeptical. But Wegener was convinced. He named the supercontinent Pangaea. (*Pan* means "all;" *gaia* means "lands.")

Today, computer models have proven Pangaea could have existed. But let's not get ahead of our story.

chapter 4

The Living Sea

Our time machine hovers in the Cambrian period. As the landmasses build and rebuild themselves, vast tidal flats surround them. The seafloor spreads, building underwater mountains. As they get bigger, they push water onto the continents. Warm, shallow seas form. See how alive they are!

The sun's radiation still makes life on dry land impossible. But the earth's warm waters suit many

Seaweed

species perfectly — especially now that algae have filled the precious liquid with oxygen. Plants like seaweed grow and bloom into undersea forests.

Kelp forests become home and pantry to worms and snails. Jellyfish with long tentacles hunt for these animals. Many soft-bodied creatures grow shells for protection. These include **mollusks**, such as clams and mussels. Others, such as trilobites and sea scorpions, grow **exoskeletons** and poisonous stingers.

22

Starfish

Creep forward a few million years. In the Devonian (di–VOH–nee–un) period, the sea is full of life. Starfish slide over corals and sponges. Sharks chase hard-scaled fish. Anemones and sea lilies sway in the warm water. These creatures look like plants with stems and petals. But they are animals. Their stems anchor them to the bottom. And their waving petals are arms that gather food.

Seawater evaporates. The vapor carries oxygen up into the atmosphere. Ozone collects and the ozone layer thickens. When it's thick enough to block radiation, plants leave the water and take root on dry land.

Anemone

The plants especially like the continents that sit on the equator. The warm, wet climate is perfect for growth. Soon the continents green with ferns and mosses. Trees first appear 365 million years ago. Sometimes the sea swells, depositing rich sediments to feed baby trees. Forests blossom into jungles.

Plants also thrive in northern Gondwana. But its southern tip sits on the South Pole. Because of the earth's tilt, the South Pole doesn't get much sun. It's so cold, big sheets of ice grow. They form the polar ice cap.

Sometimes the weather warms enough to melt the ice cap. When all that ice melts, sea levels rise. The continents flood. Floodwaters move soil, building swamps and muddy deltas.

The goo crawls with insects like scorpions and spiders. Behind them come cockroaches, crickets, and grasshoppers. Giant dragonflies buzz here and there. Beneath them, early amphibians ooze through the muck.

Dragonfly

> Amphibians are animals such as salamanders and frogs. They are comfortable both in and out of water. Many amphibians look like lizards. But they don't have scales like reptiles do. That's one reason they don't stray far from water. Their soft skin needs to stay moist.

Salamander

Most amphibians lay their eggs in water. The soft, jellylike eggs hatch into **larvae**. Frog and toad larvae are called *tadpoles*. Tadpoles breathe through gills like fish. But as they grow, they develop lungs. The process goes back millions of years.

During the Devonian period, planet Earth has seen periods of **drought**. As water sources dry up, some fish give up their gills and grow lungs. They also lose their fins. Most trade them for legs. Others crawl like snakes. These creatures are amphibians. The prehistoric type are much bigger than modern kinds. Imagine! Monster toads and giant newts are the first **vertebrates** to risk dry land.

Let's slither with them into the Carboniferous (car–buh–NIF–uh–rus) period. Everything is so green! Heavy rainfall makes trees and plants grow very fast. When they die, they don't rot. They sink to the bottom of the swampy muck. New plants grow, encouraged by heavy rain. The cycle begins again.

Layers of dead vegetation pile up. Heat and pressure turn them first into **peat**, then into coal. Some 20 percent of North America's coal forms during the Carboniferous period.

This is a time of great **tectonic** activity. Earthquakes and volcanoes build and destroy landscapes. All the landmasses move toward one another. As they push closer together, their shelves and coastlines buckle and lift. This coastal rock and soil grows into mountains. In the future, people will find seashells on top of tall mountains.

When the northern continents bump, the Appalachians are born. In the 21st century, these mountains will look like low, rounded hills. But as we move into the Permian period, the Appalachians are giant peaks. They tower over Pangaea.

Reptiles have appeared. The most advanced are therapsids (thuh–RAP–sudz). Mammals are related to these land-dwelling reptiles. Some therapsids are **vegetarians**. Others eat meat. Some are as small as rats. Others are bigger than cattle.

A strange thing happens toward the end of the Permian period. A superhot **plume** of magma rises from the earth's core. Great flows of lava erupt on the surface.

> Recent research shows the Permian problem started with a great cosmic collision. Scientists now believe an asteroid hit the earth 250 million years ago. This created the great volcanic activity that happened at that time.
>
> The evidence of this collision comes from **buckyballs**, found in Permian sediments. These tiny, hollow spheres contain outer space gases.

Huge amounts of dust, carbon dioxide, water vapor, and sulfur dioxide shoot into the air. They are trapped in the upper atmosphere. The water and sulfur dioxide form sulfuric acid. It falls back to earth as poisonous acid rain.

Then everything goes dry. Sea levels fall, draining the continental shelves. It's still hot.

In northern Pangaea, rain doesn't fall. Jungle becomes **savanna**. Forests turn into deserts. Habitats are destroyed.

Now it's a fight for survival. In the sea, 90 percent of marine species die. Some will rebound. Others, such as trilobites, never reappear.

Trilobite fossils

On land, less water means less food. Competition among animals turns fierce. Millions die. It's the worst mass extinction in our planet's history. As much as 96 percent of all life on Earth disappears during the Permian wipe-out.

Amphibians are hit hard. Without water, they have no place to lay their fragile eggs. But reptile eggs have hard shells. They are strong enough to withstand these new, dry conditions. Reptiles rise to conquer the Mesozoic (mez–uh–ZOH–ik) era. The first period in the Mesozoic era is the Triassic (try–AS–ik).

As we travel into the Triassic period, Pangaea drifts north. It sits smack on the equator. What will become Laurasia (loh–RAY–zhuh) lies to the north, Gondwana to the south. Across Pangaea, the climate is warm. No ice sheets cover the poles. Scientists think this because Triassic fossils found in Antarctica include tropical ferns.

Florida Everglades

Swampy areas that look like Florida's Everglades cover the north. These areas are filled with ferns and **horsetails**. Vast inland deserts and **conifer** forests cover the land. In what will become Arizona, the Triassic landscape looks very much like a Pacific coast redwood forest. Today, the facts are well preserved in Arizona's **Petrified** Forest National Park.

In the Triassic period, the Arizona area was marshy. The forest was a dense canopy of cone-bearing conifers. Beneath that was an understory of ferns. When the conifers died, sediment buried them. Water, rich in **silica**, penetrated the logs. Gradually, wood fibers were replaced by silica and other minerals. The trees turned to stone. Some of the minerals stained them with brilliant colors. Later, water and weather uncovered them for people to find.

Conifer forest

Reptiles rule the Triassic period. As yet, dinosaurs haven't appeared. But there are plant-eating therapsids that look like hippos and pigs. Some have moved underground. They live in holes like prairie dogs.

Meat-eating reptiles live now too. One group is called *thecodonts* (THEE–kuh–donts).

Thecodonts are about three feet long. Most of that length is tail. They use their tails for balance as they walk on their two hind legs. Their front limbs are small. They look more like arms than legs. At the end of the Triassic Period, thecodonts will become turtles, crocodiles, tiny mammals, and dinosaurs.

Some reptiles have taken to the air. They don't really fly. They glide from tree to tree, like flying squirrels. Late in the Triassic period, these small gliding reptiles will become pterosaurs (TAIR–uh–sorz).

Pterosaurs are furry and warm-blooded. They have big heads, little bodies, and long wings that are supported by finger bones. Unlike their ancestors, pterosaurs don't glide. They really fly!

Other reptiles have moved into the Triassic seas. Nothosaurs (NAH–thuh–sorz) have long bodies and tails, little heads, and legs that look like flippers. Oh, they also have very sharp teeth. They use them to snare fish.

Ichthyosaurs (IK–thee–uh–sorz) look like dolphins. They grow to 50 feet long. They like to eat giant mollusks.

Placodonts (PLAY–cuh–donz) resemble seals and prefer shellfish.

Reptiles have taken over the earth, sky, and shallow seas. These creatures quickly conquer Pangaea.

chapter 5

Sculpted by Fire and Water

Golden Gate Bridge

Have you ever seen the Golden Gate Bridge? This beautiful bridge connects San Francisco to the round hills of the Marin Headlands. The span is 9,226 feet—almost 2 miles. But the areas it connects belong at least 1,000 miles apart!

Areas that are close together but have different geological pasts are called *terranes*. Each area has one particular type of rock.

The San Francisco Bay area has ten different terranes. The Marin Headlands spent millions of years as an ocean basin before becoming part of

North America. Fossils tell scientists this terrane formed far away, probably in the middle of the Pacific.

Alcatraz Island is in the bay. It also formed in deep water, but close to shore. Alcatraz has deep sea fossils. But it also has quartz and shale. They show that the island was once part of a continent. But not *this* continent.

A little north of Alcatraz is Angel Island. The rock on Angel Island is folded. Think of how a folded blanket looks. Violent subduction does that to rock. Marin and Alcatraz show no sign of that kind of subduction. Angel Island came from someplace else.

The hills of Palo Alto have traces of coral reefs. You find those in warmer waters, close to the equator. Farther down the **peninsula**, the limestone has fossils that also came from near the equator.

The entire western U.S. is built of different terranes. From Baja California to Alaska and east to Colorado, scientists have found 200 terranes! Each is a block of the earth's crust that wouldn't subduct. Instead, it attached itself to the edge of the continent.

This happened between 100 and 200 million years ago. That's about the same time Pangaea broke apart. From the safety of our time machine, let's watch.

It's the beginning of the Jurassic (jew–RA–sik) period, 205 million years ago. Pangaea covers a large part of the earth's mantle. Heat from the core beneath can't escape. Heat energy builds up. Finally, a mantle megaplume bursts through the crust. Pangaea cracks where the northern continents, which will become Laurasia, and Gondwana first joined. Gondwana lies to the south.

These cracks ooze lava and build new mountains even as old ones crumble. The South American Andes are born in a spectacular volcanic burst. Farther north, the Rockies and Sierra Nevada also start to grow.

The Tethys Sea grows wider, forcing Laurasia and Gondwana farther apart. Where North and South America split, the Gulf of Mexico forms. To the north, New England pulls away from Africa. A valley opens in the earth's crust, becoming a baby ocean called the Atlantic. In time, Laurasia and Gondwana also rift. North America detaches from Europe. The plate bumping that joined them in the first place had built a mountain chain. As the continents divide, so do the mountains. The western side becomes the North American Catskills. The eastern slope becomes the Old Red Sandstone in northwestern Europe.

Gondwana is 400 million years old. Toward the end of the Jurassic period, it begins to break apart too. First, South America/Africa separate from Antarctica/Australia. Then South America splits from Africa. Antarctica and Australia stay joined a while longer.

Seafloor spreading moves the land masses. Africa brushes Europe, knocking off blocks of continental crust. Those pieces will settle from Spain to Arabia. The biggest chunk, which will become India, drifts toward Asia.

Other pieces of crust move toward North America's west coast. Some will become terranes in San Francisco Bay.

Earth's movements thrust huge deposits of coal out of the ground. Locked up inside the coal is carbon dioxide. As wind and weather work on the coal, carbon dioxide is released. Remember, carbon dioxide holds heat. It builds up in the atmosphere and the world gets warmer.

The earth keeps bubbling new crust. Sea levels rise. Inland seas are born as water invades dry land. Warm winds blow across the water, picking up moisture and turning it into rain. Rain! Parched areas bloom and grow lush. Conifers tower over ginkgoes, cycads (palms), and

Palms

shrubs. Ferns and horsetails form a dense carpet beneath the trees. Food is abundant.

In this inviting world, the first dinosaurs roam.

chapter 6

Dino Detectives

People's fascination with "terrible" (*dino*) "lizards" (*sauros*) began two centuries ago. In the late 1700s, a huge skeleton was unearthed in New Jersey. People were curious. But they had no clue what it was. And those giant fossil footprints nearby? Who even wanted to think about what creature made those?

In 1822, more bones were discovered in England. Those bones were carefully examined by top British scientists. English **naturalist** William Buckley published the first scientific account of a dinosaur in 1824. He named the 30-foot monster *megalosaurus* (MAY–guh–luh–sor–us).

Since then, dinosaurs have been unearthed on every continent. The scientists who study them are called *paleontologists* (pay–lee–un–TAH–luh–jists). Their work is much like detective work. Since they have no live dinosaurs to study, they must dig up clues.

What kind of clues? Fossil clues, of course. Fossilized bones hint how dinosaurs looked. Fossilized footprints show how they moved. Fossilized dung shows what they ate. Fossilized nests show how they reproduced and raised their young.

These fossil clues may answer old questions. Or they may raise new ones. Sometimes they lead to arguments. Once in a while, they create heated competition among dino detectives.

> In 1858, American Joseph Leidy unearthed a dinosaur skeleton in Haddonfield, New Jersey. Like earlier finds, Leidy's "duckbill" was found in an area with a mild, moist climate.
>
> American scientists O. C. Marsh and E. D. Cope focused instead on the arid North American west. The area had large stretches of exposed rock. As the two men raced to find dinosaurs, they became fierce rivals.
>
> Marsh's important discoveries were found in areas that include Canon City in Colorado and Como Bluff, Wyoming. The Como Bluff site yielded a staggering assortment of dinosaurs, tiny to terrible. More importantly, he sparked interest in the ancient reptiles.
>
> Cope's explorations carried him farther than Marsh's. He found a wider variety of fossils, but not as many dinosaurs. His most important dinosaur discoveries were in the badlands of Montana.

Early paleontologists used simple tools like picks and shovels. Since the science was so new, they had to guess about what they were finding. Often, they guessed wrong. For instance, the first fossilized dinosaur footprints were discovered in 1802. Some people guessed they were made by giant, extinct birds.

Many dinosaur footprints do look like giant bird tracks. This led to a hot dino debate. Did birds descend from dinosaurs?

Most dino detectives say yes. Many clues seem to support the idea.

Triceratops

- Baby dinosaurs grew quickly. Baby birds grow quickly. Baby lizards do not.
- A fragment of triceratops (try–SAIR–uh–tops) DNA (the "blueprint" of every living thing) matches a fragment of turkey DNA. This doesn't mean they looked alike. But it does link the two.
  - Fossilized theropod (THIR–uh–pod) footprints also connect to turkeys. The prints were left behind in soft, mucky mudflats. Turkeys running in soft mud leave almost identical tracks.
  - Fossilized nests show mother oviraptors (oh–vi–RAP–tors) and troodons (true–OH–donz), both meat-eating dinosaurs, sat on their eggs like birds. Scientists don't know if this was to keep the eggs warm, shade them, or protect them from predators.

- Fossil evidence shows nesting troodons brought food back to the nest for their hatchlings, just like birds do.
- A well-preserved troodon had featherlike structures along its back.
- Analysis of dino **keratin** showed it is identical to the keratin found in feathers. But it is not the same as the keratin found in reptile scales.

Today, the study of fossil footprints is called *ichnology* (ik–NAH–luh–jee). Ichnology answers questions like these. How far did dinosaurs travel? Did they move in herds or alone? Did they walk on all fours or sprint on two feet? Did big meat-eaters hunt singly? Or—scary thought—in packs? Speaking of big **carnivores**, here's one for *Jurassic Park* fans. Could T-Rexes have run 35 miles per hour, like in that movie?

Tyrannosaurus

No way, say ichnologists. Top speed for big tyrannosauruses (tuh–RAN–uh–sor–us–ez) was around 22 miles per hour. Their **stride** was between six and seven feet. That's five to seven times the length of their feet. This **formula** works for any dinosaur that walked on two feet.

Modern dino detectives use many new tools to search for clues. To study keratin, they use an ultra-sensitive electron microscope. Instead of lenses, this special microscope uses energy beams to magnify things. This gives a better look at the structure of things like keratin.

CAT scanners use pencil thin X-ray beams to look inside human bodies. Then they send the information to computers to draw accurate 3-D pictures of what they see. CT scanners are like CAT scanners, but they produce more detailed pictures.

Paleontologists use CT scanners to look inside fossils. Computers use the information they receive to show how dinosaur bones fit together or how hollow they were. By looking inside a skull, scientists can tell how big a dinosaur's brain was. They can also put all that information together. Then they build models of how dinosaurs looked and moved.

CT scans have led to some new ideas about the big meat-eating dinosaurs.
- Scans of T-Rex skulls show their sense of smell was better than their eyesight. Some scientists think that means T-Rexes were more **scavengers** than hunters. Why? Because hunters need keen eyesight. And scavengers "sniff out" their dead meat meals. T-Rexes may have been dinosaur buzzards!
- T-Rexes' cousins, allosauruses (ah–luh–SOR–us–es) had 80 razor-sharp teeth. But scans show they had weak bites. They also had very strong skulls. Researchers think they head-slammed their prey instead of snapping their jaws around the victims.

Of course, even the best equipment doesn't answer every question. And different scientists may look at the same clues and get different answers.

One of the biggest dino debates is whether they were warm-blooded like birds or cold-blooded like reptiles. In 1999, researchers claimed a CT scan gave them the first image of a fossilized dinosaur heart. They said the scan showed the heart had four chambers, like warm-blooded animals' hearts.

Other scientists reviewed the scans. They decided it wasn't a heart at all, just a blob of mud. But a group of heart surgeons agreed the scan seemed to show a heart. Still others said even if it *is* a dinosaur heart, the four chambers don't prove anything. Crocodiles, which are reptiles, have four-chamber hearts. But they work differently than four-chamber mammal hearts.

It will take more clues to settle the debate. But that's what science is all about.

Every year brings new discoveries. Most are in North America. And that's where our story continues, 200 million years ago.

39

chapter 7

T-Rexes in Texas

Jurassic America. What a picture! North America is still part of Laurasia. Yes, this continent is in one piece, but just barely. A narrow strip of land connects what will become Alaska and Mongolia, China. On the other side, North America joins Europe through Greenland.

A great inland sea covers the Cordilleran region. This area extends over the western third of the continent.

In the 21st century, scientists will discover seashells in the Utah desert. They will find prehistoric fish encased in Wyoming rock. And the bones of ancient crocodiles and turtles will turn up in the badlands of South Dakota.

The water stretches from the Arctic to the Gulf of Mexico, splitting Laurasia in two. The water retreats to the north several times. Then it pushes south again. This is due to regular changes in the weather.

Pterodactyl

The earth now has seasons. Sometimes it's wet. Sometimes it's dry. The inland sea is warm and shallow. Ichthyosaurs swim with plesiosaurs (PLEE–see–uh–sorz). These meat-eaters grow 50 feet long. Some have long necks and small heads. Others have huge heads, almost 1/4 their body length. Plesiosaurs have flippers. These animals often creep onshore to sun themselves. To dive, they swallow stones.

Other carnivores live in these waters. Check out the marine crocodiles. These giant saltwater crocs have flippers instead of legs. They are aggressive hunters.

Plesiosaur

Overhead, skin-winged pterosaurs soar. Then they dive, spearing fish with spiked teeth. Some have grown tails. Others, pterodactyls (tair–uh–DAK–tulz), do not have tails. Early birds have also taken wing. They have bones, teeth, and claws like their therapsid ancestors. But they have feathers.

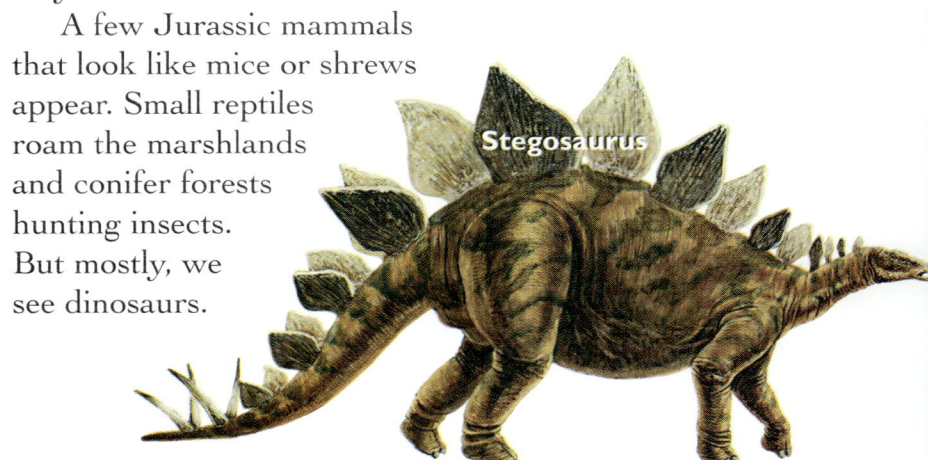

A few Jurassic mammals that look like mice or shrews appear. Small reptiles roam the marshlands and conifer forests hunting insects. But mostly, we see dinosaurs.

Stegosaurus

Some dinosaurs are **herbivores**. Stegosauruses (steg–uh–SOR–us–es) are about 30 feet long. They have little heads and tiny brains. They plod along, searching for the plants that make up their diet. These dinosaurs aren't smart and they aren't fast. Good thing they have those armored plates for protection!

Apatosaurus

Brachiosaurus

Sauropods (SOR–uh–podz) tower above the stegosauruses. These giant plant-eaters are the biggest creatures ever to roam the earth. Sauropods walk on all fours. But they can stand on their hind legs to reach the tallest treetops.

They have gigantic tails, super long necks, and tiny heads with brains no bigger than cats' brains. They aren't bright or quick either. But they are just too big for most predators to bother.

Apatosauruses (ah–PAH–tuh–sor–us–es) were once called *brontosauruses* (BRAUN–tuh–sor–us–es). These 80-foot-long sauropods live on both supercontinents.

The sauropod family also includes 87-foot diplodocuses (duh–PLAH–duh–cus–uz). They are longer than apatosauruses. But they are slender and weigh less.

We see camarasauruses (kuh–MAIR–uh–sor–us–es). At 59 feet long, they are the smallest Jurassic sauropods. Camarasauruses have strong tails and short necks. They graze on grass in the shallow marshlands of the western U.S.

Finally, we find 80-ton brachiosauruses (BRAK–e–uh–sor–us–es). They are 40 times bigger than elephants and stand as tall as four-story buildings.

For many years, scientists believed brachiosauruses were the biggest creatures to ever roam the earth. But researchers have unearthed bigger sauropod skeletons. First came a 100-foot-long supersaurus (SUE–per–sor–us). Then a 110-foot ultrasaurus (UL–trah–sor–us) was found. And in New Mexico, 125-foot seismosaurus (SIZE–muh–sor–us) was uncovered.

In eastern Oklahoma, dino detectives have uncovered sauroposeidon (sor–uh–poh–SIGH–dun). They weighed about 60 tons, a little less than some of their cousins. But they had the longest necks of all of them. Sauroposeidons munched leaves from trees as tall as six-story buildings!

Velociraptor

Fierce carnivorous dinosaurs terrorize the Jurassic period. Coelurosaurs (COH–lur–uh–sorz) are only about seven feet long. But they're lightweight and have lightning-fast speed. They sprint after prey on their hind legs, using their large tails for balance. Velociraptors (vuh–LAH–suh–rap–torz) are coelurosaurs.

Coelurosaurs are especially scary because they hunt in packs. Together, these dinosaurs can take down victims ten times their size.

> Modern reptiles are cold-blooded. They move slowly because their blood can't give their muscles enough oxygen for active movement.
>
> Coelurosaurs and other dinosaurs moved quickly. Many scientists now believe these reptiles were warm-blooded.
>
> Others think at least some dinosaurs had the "best of both worlds." Research shows theropods may have been cold-blooded. While at rest, their bodies conserved energy. But theropods were fast, dangerous predators. When chasing prey, they had energy to spare.
>
> The warm-blooded versus cold-blooded theory is one hot dino debate.

The most savage Jurassic predators are the early carnosaurs (CAR–nuh–sorz). These "flesh lizards" include megalosauruses. These 30-foot monsters walk upright. Their hands have three fingers tipped with nasty claws. Megalosauruses live on both Laurasia and Gondwana, but they prefer eastern Laurasia. Many of their bones will be found in England.

Their cousins, allosauruses, wander western North America. Allosauruses are 40 feet long and weigh 2 tons. They walk on stout hind legs, with huge birdlike feet. Wicked claws, huge jaws, and **serrated** teeth make allosauruses the Jurassic period's biggest, "baddest" dinosaurs.

At minus 140 million, we move into the Cretaceous (kri–TAY–shus) period. This name means "chalk." Cretaceous rock is filled with chalky deposits loaded with tiny shells. The chalk is left behind as inland seas retreat.

As this period gets underway, conditions still favor reptiles. New species include turtles and snakes. Amphibians, such as frogs and salamanders, appear again. Herons, gulls, and plovers swoop after fish. Opossumlike mammals thrive in trees, such as oaks and hickories.

Dinosaurs also flourish. The sauropods, chewing tree leaves, are still the biggest. Triceratops plod through the undergrowth. They get their name from their three horns. One is over the nose and the other two are on their foreheads. Bony plates protect their necks and the backs of their large heads.

Ankylosauruses (AN–kuh–luh–sor–us–es) have even more armor. These elephant-sized dinosaurs have rows of bony plates covering their backs and heads.

One type of these dinosaurs are ankylosaurids (AN–kuh–luh–sor–idz). They have large clubs on the ends of their tails. They use the clubs to defend themselves. Another type, nodosaurids, do not have tail clubs. But they have large spikes sticking out from their necks.

Ankylosauruses aren't choosy. Their fossilized remains will be found from Africa to Colorado.

Herds of iguanadons (i–GWAH–nuh–donz)

Iguanadon

Allosaurus

walk both upright and on all fours. These large herbivores sometimes reach 25 feet in length. When they stand on their hind legs, they are often 15 feet tall. They have long, flat heads, which end in horny beaks. Their teeth are almost exactly like those of iguana lizards in the future. That's why scientists will give them this name. Iguanadons prefer eastern Laurasia.

Late in the Cretaceous period, duck-billed dinosaurs appear. These strange reptiles also travel in herds and migrate seasonally. Duckbills do swim, using their large, flat tails for paddles. But they do not live in the water, as scientists will believe for a while. Later research shows duckbills chew on tree leaves, not underwater vegetation.

Cretaceous predators are awesome. A species of allosauruses, gigantosauruses (jeye–GAN–tuh–sor–us–es) rule in Gondwana. But in Laurasia, the awesome tyrannosauruses reign supreme. To the east, another type of allosauruses, Albertosauruses (al–BURR–tuh–sor–us–es), dominate. But out west, it's T-Rexes all the way.

These 50-foot, 14,000-pound monsters have massive heads. Their teeth are seven inches long.

Their arms are so tiny that T-Rexes don't really use them for anything. Instead, they hold their prey with their huge hind legs while ripping meat with their giant teeth. Their favorite food is triceratops. But these three-horned dinosaurs can certainly defend themselves. So, T-Rexes must use strategy to hunt.

> Did the big carnivorous dinosaurs hunt in packs? New evidence says maybe. Most tyrannosaurus skeletons have been found singly. But a Canadian site has revealed what seems to be a pack, including young and old tyrannosauruses.
>
> Dino hunter Phil Currie discovered this surprising evidence. He believes young tyrannosauruses, which were fast, may have cut a single dinosaur from a herd. Then they chased the prey toward larger, slower tyrannosauruses. The bigger beasts could then use their massive jaws and teeth to capture the victim. Discovery of a new species of allosauruses also seems to show this type of cooperative hunting.

chapter 8

Dinosaur Doomsday

So here we hover in the Cretaceous period. The entire planet enjoys warm temperatures. **Coal swamps** are found in Alaska and forests near the North Pole. Dinosaurs prosper in the tropical climate. Yet, we know they won't survive the period. What happens over the next 75 million years?

Scientists have many ideas about the great dinosaur die-off. Most believe one of three theories.

- Dinosaurs were too stupid to survive.
- Dinosaurs were too big to survive.
- Dinosaur eggs were eaten by mammal predators.

But these three theories seem to have major flaws.

Dinosaurs ruled the earth for 160 million years. The more we learn about them, the more we see how adaptable they were. Scientists can find no evidence that these animals were too stupid or too big to survive.

Mammal predators probably did eat eggs. But dinosaurs laid eggs in great numbers. Many were doting parents and guarded their nests against intruders. There were simply too many dinosaurs and not enough mammals for the egg-stealing theory to hold up.

Finally, none of these theories explains why other species, both plant and animal, died off at the same time. The Cretaceous extinction was as widespread as the Permian extinction. Scientists looked for similar changes in the environment. The evidence they uncovered led to new ideas about "Dinosaur Doomsday." Earth movements. Continental drift. Volcanic activity. Mountain building. Climate changes. **Isolation** of species. One big meteorite. All played at least minor roles in the Cretaceous drama.

Look around. The Cretaceous period is a highly volcanic time. Across the planet, new mountains and islands are born. America's west coast is fringed with volcanoes. They erupt again and again. The cooling layers become the Sierra Nevada. Farther east, the Rockies also grow.

All this erupting sends clouds of ash into the atmosphere. The earth gets less sunshine and cools. This is especially true at the planet's poles.

Laurasia's and Gondwana's pieces begin to move farther apart. They carry plants and animals into different climate zones. As the pieces drift closer to the poles, their weather changes radically. Winters become more severe.

Rainfall patterns also change. Swamps become deserts. Dry grasslands become mud holes.

Many species, including some dinosaurs, die off.

New species replace the old ones. They adapt to the cooler, drier weather. But they can't spread throughout the world or even across the continents. Growing oceans and mountains stand in their way.

Plants and animals now change in their isolated pockets. Living things are affected by their environment—temperature, air pressure, light, and food. These things decide how and where different species develop. Many of the later dinosaurs develop only in Asia/America. Despite the climate change, most do well. At least for a while.

Flowering plants and trees replace cycads and broad-leaved conifers. Many of these new plants develop poisonous, bitter-tasting **alkaloids**. Some animals won't eat them. Others do and suffer the consequences.

> Some scientists blame the dinosaur die-off on alkaloid poisoning. They believe dinosaurs were never able to taste the alkaloids' bitter flavor. As the plant-eaters died, so did the carnivores that fed on them.
>
> The alkaloid problem probably did contribute to Dinosaur Doomsday. But it was not the only reason. Dinosaurs and flowering plants successfully shared the earth for 60 million years. And the theory still does not explain why so many other Cretaceous species died.

As flowering plants take over, a whole new **fauna** follows. These insects and birds help **pollinate** plants. Mammals, reptiles and amphibians adapt to eat the new insects and birds.

Our time machine has reached minus 70 million, the beginning of Cenozoic (see-nuh-ZOH-ik) era. Everything seems in order. And then, boom! A meteorite, about 6 miles wide, crashes into Mexico. The impact pushes it 18½ miles deep into the earth. It creates a crater that is 112 miles across.

> Besides planets and their moons, countless chunks of rocky debris orbit the sun. These are meteorites. Many have crashed into the earth over its long history.
>
> You can still see the crater at Chicxulub (cheek–HOO–loob) in Mexico's Yucatan Peninsula. The Chicxulub meteorite isn't solely responsible for the Cretaceous devastation. But it definitely dealt a major blow to species already struggling to survive.

Firestorms rage, burning plants and animals. But flames don't kill most of them. Dust clouds and smoke completely block the sun. They are laced with great amounts of sulfur. As in the Permian period, water vapor and sulfur combine to form deadly acid rain.

The earth's seas become acid baths. Algae and plankton are wiped out. Sea creatures that eat these plants die off, followed by marine predators.

A similar chain of events takes place on dry land. Without sunshine, a dark, eerie "winter" spreads over planet Earth. It lasts for many months. Plants that use sun to make food die. Without those plants, many herbivores die. Without those herbivores, carnivores die. Dinosaur Doomsday.

chapter 9

Mammals Take Over

The earth does not recover overnight. It takes a million years, give or take a few. Slowly, the meteorite's dust cloud filters back down through the atmosphere. During the Cenozoic era, the climate becomes tropical again.

Figs and magnolias bloom in Alaska. The Dakotas have palm trees and monster crocodiles. Greenland has no snow, just giant redwood trees. It would be perfect for dinosaurs. But they're gone. Many are buried in ash-heavy sediments. Their bones have become fossils. In some places, salty sediments preserve their bodies like **mummies**.

Fast forward into the Eocene (EE–uh–seen) epoch. With no dinosaurs to eat them, forests flourish. Lush undergrowth offers the perfect **habitat** for "modern" mammals. Older mammals like shrews and hedgehogs remain. But new species have joined them.

Bats cruise the night sky, hunting insects. Rabbits, camels, and tiny horses hop, trot, and lope across open stretches. In the trees are squirrellike rodents and weasellike predators.

Mammals are warm-blooded. Their body temperature stays the same, whether it's cold or hot. Mammals bear their young live and nurse them. Mammals breathe air and have hair.

Early **primates** also hang out in the trees. These are the distant ancestors of apes. They don't look much like monkeys, though—more like lemurs. But their large brains and grasping hands set them apart from other mammals.

Our time machine creeps forward. Africa bumps Eurasia, closing off the eastern end of the Tethys Sea. The water that remains is now the Mediterranean Sea. The plate bumping jump-starts the Alps and Himalayas.

Meanwhile, the North American plate climbs over the Pacific plate. The collision cracks North America's western edge. This crack in the continental crust is California's San Andreas fault.

Lemur

Faults are cracks in the earth's crust where the rocks on either side move. Cracks without movement are called *joints*. Faults might be a few inches or thousands of miles long. Faults create several unique landforms.
- A scarp is a cliff that rises on one side of the fault.

- A graben is a low rock block with scarps on either side.
- A rift valley is a valley made up of a graben. The Great Rift Valley in Africa is 3,000 miles long.
- A basin is a sunken block of rock.
- A range is a raised block of rock. The basin and range region in the southwestern part of the United States is made up of hundreds of landforms.

The Sierra Nevada grow taller. Farther north, the Cascade Range bubbles up. Farther south, blocks of the earth sink and uplift, in a regular up-and-down pattern. This is the basin and range structure of the southwestern United States.

As the planet heaves, it coughs up rock from deep within. Remember how uplifted coal released carbon dioxide, warming the planet? This rock does the opposite. It absorbs carbon dioxide. As the atmosphere loses carbon dioxide, the earth gets drier. And colder. The trend continues until the Pleistocene (PLY–stuh–seen) Ice Age.

Ice ages happen about every 150 million years. The atmosphere cools, and temperatures drop. The ocean gets cold, and glaciers spread across the northern parts of the world.

After a million years or so, things swing back the other way. Temperatures warm, glaciers melt. Huge amounts of water gush across the continents, carving out canyons and valleys. The water ends up in the oceans. Sea levels rise.

Ice ages seem to be caused by the rotation of our Milky Way galaxy. Each rotation takes 300 million years, changing our planet's climate twice.

At minus 38 million, we move into the Oligocene (AH–lig–oh–seen) epoch. In Europe and here in North America, the climate is still subtropical. But an ice sheet covers Antarctica. The polar forests have disappeared. In their place is frozen **tundra**.

Different animals adapt to each region. In areas with more trees, we find more tree-dwellers. Here in North America, we find more grazing animals. Some resemble their modern relatives. Others look weird and kind of scary. One has a horse head; camel body; and long, narrow claws. Another looks like a giant rhino. But these strange animals soon become extinct.

Others thrive and adapt. We see early dogs. These are the ancestors of modern dogs and wolves. Bears, raccoons, pandas, and badgers appear. Cats, including the saber-toothed variety, are also seen.

Hoofed animals range widely across North America.

Saber-toothed Tiger

56

Little camels the size of sheep are here. And so are pigs, both miniature and giant. Early antelopes and horses have developed long legs to help them outrun predators. More importantly, their teeth and stomachs have changed. Instead of leaves, they now can eat grass.

Why is that important? The changing climate favors grass over forests. Grass tolerates drought—and being nibbled. It regrows quickly after being chewed. In fact, grazing makes grass spread faster. Grass needs grazers. Grazers need grass. The win-win situation ensures the survival of both.

Other mammals will never outrun predators. So they grow *really* big. Or develop *really* thick hides. Some, like mammoths, do both. In response, some carnivores grow *really* big teeth. Saber-toothed cats can bite through just about anything.

Mammals are simply more intelligent than the reptiles that ruled before them. That's why they do so well. For some species, survival means **cunning**. This is important for animals that stalk prey.

For others, survival means safety in numbers. Some animals move in herds. Primates and whales form tight societies. On dry land or in the sea, cooperation is the key to their success.

At minus 24 million, we find ourselves in the Miocene (MY–uh–seen) epoch. It is definitely colder now. More and more forests have turned to grassland. Vast savannas stretch across North America and Africa.

In Africa, a new species has appeared. These apelike primates are the first of their kind. They move on all fours through the tropical rain forest.

In East Africa, different apes live in the trees. These early orangutans cross a land bridge into Europe, then move on to Asia. One day, their relatives will be found in places like Sumatra.

Those apes have really great teeth! Seriously, their tooth enamel has grown thicker. They can now eat hard fruits and nuts. That's important because the cooler, drier earth has less food for the animals.

chapter

The Very First Americans

At minus 2,000,000 years, *h. sapiens* (humans) make their appearance on the scene. Whether they first appear in Africa or southern Asia is another hot debate. Either way, larger brains give people a definite edge. They quickly learn to use tools and conquer fire. Now they can cook food and defeat the frigid Ice Age temperatures.

Humans are also travelers. They spread throughout Africa, Europe, and Asia. Each place has a different environment. So humans develop differently, depending on where they live.

The humans that settle in Europe begin to resemble modern Europeans—narrow faces and jutting chins. Those that move on into Asia develop different features—rounder faces and heavier cheekbones.

Their languages begin to differ too. Oh, yes, these primitive people speak. Communication is key to humans' survival. They find safety in numbers. And so they gather together. Most live in tribes of 30 or more. In some areas, they become cave-dwellers and begin to decorate their cave walls.

Galloping across the walls are horses, bison, and deer. These animal drawings are beautifully painted with natural dyes. Chewed twigs and feathers serve as paintbrushes. The details are incredible, even thousands of years later. It seems these people believe in magic. They paint the animals to gain power over them and ensure successful hunting.

Replica of Lascaux cave painting of a bull and horse

Some humans survive by gathering nuts, fruits, and insects to eat. Others learn to catch fish. Still others are mighty hunters. Mammoth is their favorite meat. Humans chase these woolly beasts across Europe and Asia. As they travel, they set up camps, complete with tents. If a cold spell hits, they burrow into hillsides or make skin huts.

Mammoths

Humans spread throughout the Old World. Now they find their way to Australia and America. Here, we must shift the time machine into neutral. For now, new scientific debate begins.

Scientists have long believed humans followed the mammoths north into Siberia. From there, they crossed a land bridge into Alaska. The strip of land in the Bering Strait lifted as sea levels fell in the Pleistocene Ice Age. This happened, the old story goes, 12,000 years ago.

From Alaska, humans quickly moved south. Wearing animal skins and carrying spears, these hunters made their way across the continent. They left behind spearpoints with an unusual shape. Within 500 years, humans had scattered throughout North America. These were the ancestors of modern Native Americans.

This idea is known as the Clovis theory. The name comes from the discovery of an unusual spearpoint in Clovis, New Mexico. The 1933 find was the first, but not the last. Clovis points have been unearthed all across America. The dirt around them dates back 11,500 years.

Nothing older was found for many years. Scientists settled on the Clovis theory. Some still believe that's how—and when—people came to America.

Anthropologist Tom Dillehay used to believe in Clovis. "I grew up in Texas where the Clovis sites were abundant," he said. "I was generally sold on the theory, although my mind was open to other ideas."

In 1977, Dillehay was teaching at a college in southern Chile. A student brought him a cow molar, which actually belonged to a mastodon. That tooth led Dillehay to a peat bog in Monte Verde, Chile. He and his researchers found mastodon bones, butchering tools, and a whole lot more.

The peat had preserved a campsite. Some 30 hunters had lived there 12,500 years ago. Nearby digs have revealed even older tools. Maybe as old as 30,000 years.

"What makes Monte Verde so incredible," said Dillehay, "is the preservation of organic remains—hides, chunks of mastodon meat, medicinal herbs. All at least 1,500 years older than Clovis. And some are probably way older than that."

People were in Chile 13,000 years ago. If they wandered down from Siberia, it would have taken them thousands of years to get to South America. That means humans probably arrived in North America 15,000 to 20,000 years ago. Or longer.

> Other archaeological finds support the "pre-Clovis theory."
> - Pennsylvania researchers have found a prehistoric "campground" at Meadowcroft Rock Shelter. Ancient peoples paused beneath the tall cliff, where their campfires were protected. The leftover charcoal dates back 17,000 years.

- Wisconsin researchers have uncovered mammoth "butcher shops." Mammoth bones and ivory tusks bear the marks of ancient cutting tools. The bones date back 13,500 years.
- Virginia researchers have found a mastodon butcher site. Bones and stone tools, including an ivory polisher, were found in a 14,000-year-old sediment layer.
- Canadian researchers discovered the "Bluefish Caves." Inside, they found the bones of butchered mammoths. These dated back 15,500 to 20,000 years. And there were tools made of bone, some 23,500 years old.

Other evidence backs up the pre-Clovis notion. There's a problem with language. From Alaska to the tip of South America, Native Americans speak 143 different languages. They are as different from one another as Chinese and English. And that makes the Clovis theory impossible.

Say a tribe of mammoth hunters migrates from Siberia. The tribe splits in two and each half wanders in different directions. They speak the same language when they split. Over time, they start to sound different. But it would take 6,000 years before they couldn't understand each other at all.

So how long would it take for 140 languages to evolve from a single tongue? One language expert estimated 60,000 years.

Many scientists now believe people came to America in waves. They may not have all come on foot. And they may not have all come by way of Siberia.

It now seems America may always have been a "melting pot."

"Spirit Caveman" lived 9,400 years ago. His remains were found in western Nevada in 1940. He was a fisherman, not a mammoth hunter. He did not wear animal skins, but a carefully woven blanket. And he did not look Siberian or Native American. He looked Indonesian or maybe European.

In 1996, two kids in Washington State stumbled upon "Kennewick Man." At first, **forensic** investigators thought the skeleton belonged to a European settler. Imagine their surprise when they found a 9,000-year-old spearpoint lodged in his hip!

People who studied Kennewick Man's remains created this image on the computer to show what he may have looked like.

The spearpoint belonged to Washington's prehistoric "Cascade People." Kennewick Man did not. There were at least two ancient cultures on the Columbia River. And sometimes they clashed!

Other prehistoric skeletons have been found throughout North and South America. Of a dozen studied, only two seem to have Siberian ancestors. Others look Polynesian or like Japan's native Ainu people. DNA tests have shown at least three ancient cultures migrated to America. The earliest probably arrived 30,000 years ago.

So how did they get here? Thirty thousand years ago, the Siberia-Alaska route was covered by glaciers. The ice sheets started to melt around minus 18,000. Crossing them on foot would have been nearly impossible.

But what if people came by boat? Humans arrived in Australia 55,000 years ago. The only way to get there was by boat. Could the very first Americans have arrived by kayak?

It's possible. They could have hugged the Bering ice sheets, stopping when necessary. Fish and sea mammals like seals offered plentiful "fast food."

Once people got to America, they could have cruised on down the coastline to South America. A number of early societies flourished along the coast. People lived in the Channel Islands near Santa Barbara, California, over 10,000 years ago. And seafarers lived in Peru at minus 11,000.

Some proof may never be found. Coastal dwellers may have camped on continental shelves, which were exposed when sea levels dropped. As glaciers melted and sea levels rose, their tools and campfires would have been covered with water.

Okay, if humans skirted Pacific glaciers, could they have crossed the Atlantic the same way? Some scientists think so. An ice sheet spanned the Atlantic between England and Nova Scotia. It would have a been a long, dangerous trip. But not impossible.

"If people moved along the fringes of the Beringia ice sheets," said Tom Dillehay, "they could have done the same on the north Atlantic side too. I'm not sold on the idea. More research is necessary. But I keep that door cautiously open."

"That door" could explain how pre-Clovis tools have been unearthed in Virginia. They look like tools used in Spain about 24,000 years ago. It might also explain why no Clovis points have ever been found in Alaska or Siberia. If Clovis people came that way, you'd expect to find them.

However people reached America, it suited them fine. They spread out, settled in, and started "Native American" families. Game was plentiful. The weather was good. And if it got bad, they could always build a fire.

Before long, mammoths, saber-toothed tigers, and giant pigs vanished like shadows. But humans were here to stay.

A FINAL WORD

Our **chronometer** reads "today." The time machine has taxied to a stop. It's definitely been a rocket ride. Hope you found some answers. Hope you have more questions. That's what history is all about.

By learning about the past, we discover our future.

GLOSSARY

abyss	bottomless pit or great space
alkaloid	colorless, bitter substance found in plants
anthropologist	person who studies humans, their lives, and their history
atmosphere	mass of air surrounding the earth
buckyball	molecule of a form of pure carbon
buoyant	having the ability to float
carnivore	meat-eating animal
chronometer	very accurate timepiece
coal swamp	wet place where peat (see glossary entry) and, later, coal formed
compress	to become smaller in size and volume by squeezing
conifer	evergreen tree that produces pine cones
core	center
cunning	skill or knowledge
debate	discussion between opposing sides of an issue
drench	to wet thoroughly
drought	period of dryness
equator	imaginary line around the middle of the earth where the climate is very hot
erosion	act of wearing away by the sun, wind, and water
exhale	breath or vapor (see glossary entry)
exoskeleton	bony or horny outside covering of an animal
extinct	gone forever
fauna	animal life

forensic	relating to or dealing with the use of scientific knowledge for legal problems
formula	general rule or principle
giddy	dizzy
gravity	invisible force that pulls toward the center of the earth
habitat	place where animals and plants live
herbivore	plant-eating animal
horsetail	thin-leafed plant that spreads from the roots
isolation	act of remaining alone
keratin	sulfur that contains proteins that form the basis of horny tissue such as hair and nails
larva	the immature form that hatches from the egg of many insects
magma	molten rock within the earth
marine	relating to the sea
mollusk	animal with a soft body enclosed in a shell, such as a snail or a clam
mummy	body treated for burial with preservatives in the manner of the ancient Egyptians
naturalist	one who believes that there are scientific laws to explain everything
oceanic	having to do with the ocean
peat	soil that has been formed by the breakdown of vegetation with water and heat
peninsula	portion of land nearly surrounded by water
petrified	relating to organic matter changed into stone

plume	column of smoke or gases
pollen	small spores in a seed plant usually in the form of fine dust
pollinate	to transfer pollen (see glossary entry) from one plant part to another
prehistoric	relating to times before written history
primate	order of mammals consisting of humans, apes, monkeys, and others
recede	to go back
rift valley	long valley between two faults formed by the depression in the earth's crust
savanna	treeless plain
scavenger	animal that eats other animals that are already dead
sediment	matter that settles to the bottom of a liquid
serrated	having a sharp notched or toothed edge
silica	compound found in quartz, opal, or sand
species	distinct type of plant or animal
sphere	globe or ball
stride	long step
tectonic	having to do with the structure of the crust of a planet or moon
timescale	arrangement of events used as a measure of a period of history or geological time
tundra	treeless plain found in the Arctic regions
vapor	matter, such as smoke or fog, that hangs in the air
vegetarian	one who only eats vegetables
vertebrate	animal with a backbone
watershed	region bounded by a divide and draining to a particular body of water

INDEX

Acasta, Canada, 17
Africa, 19, 20, 21, 32, 46, 54, 55, 58, 59
Alaska, 4, 20, 31, 40, 49, 53, 61, 63, 65, 66
Albertosaurus, 47
Alcatraz Island, 31
allosaurus, 38, 45, 47, 48
amphibian, 24–25, 27, 46, 52
Angel Island, 31
ankylosaurid, 46
ankylosaurus, 46
Antarctica, 4, 19, 20, 21, 27, 32, 56
apatosaurus, 42, 43
Archaean eon, 14, 15, 16–17, 18–19
Asia, 19, 32, 51, 54, 58, 59, 60, 61
Atlantic Ocean, 21, 32, 66
Australia, 19, 21, 32, 61, 65
Bacon, Sir Francis, 21
Bluefish Caves, 63
brachiosaurus, 43–44
brontosaurus, 43
Buckley, William, 34
camarasaurus, 43
Cambrian period, 14, 15, 19, 22
Canon City, Colorado, 35
Carboniferous period, 14, 25
carnosaur, 45
Cascade People, 65
Cenozoic era, 14, 52, 53
China, 19, 40
Chicxulub, Mexico, 52
Clovis, New Mexico, 61
Clovis theory, 61–62, 66
coelurosaur, 44–45
Como Bluff, Wyoming, 35

Cope, E. D., 35
Cordilleran region, 40
Cretaceous period, 14, 45–50, 51, 52
Currie, Phil, 48
Devonian period, 14, 23, 25
Dillehay, Tom, 62, 66
diplodocus, 43
duckbill, 35, 47
Eocene epoch, 14, 53–56
Europe, 19, 20, 32, 40, 54, 56, 58, 59, 60, 61, 64
fossil, 9–10, 12, 15, 20, 21, 27, 31, 35, 36, 37, 38, 46, 53
geological timescale, 13–14, 70
gigantosaurus, 47
Glen Tilt, Scotlan, 10, 11
Gondwana, 19, 20, 24, 27, 32, 45, 47, 50
Greenland, 4, 40, 53
Gulf of Mexico, 32, 41
Haddonfield, New Jersey, 35
Holmes, Arthur, 13
human, 59–66
Hutton, James, 10–12
ichthyosaur, 29, 41
iguanadon, 46–47
India, 19, 21, 32
Jurassic period, 14, 32, 40, 42, 43, 44, 45
Kennewick Man, 64
Laurasia, 27, 32, 40, 41, 45, 47, 50
Leidy, Joseph, 35
mammal, 26, 29, 39, 42, 46, 49, 52–54, 56–58, 65
mammoth, 57, 61, 63, 64, 66
Marin Headlands, 30–31

Marsh, O. C., 35
mastodon, 62, 63
Meadowcroft Rock Shelter, 62
megalosaurus, 34, 45
Mesozoic era, 14, 27
Miocene epoch, 14, 58
Monte Verde, Chile, 62
mountains
    Alps, 54
    Appalachians, 26
    Andes, 32
    Cascades, 55
    Catskills, 32
    Himalayas, 54
    Old Red Sandstone, 32
    Rockies, 32, 50
    Sierra Nevada, 32, 50, 55
nodosaurid, 46
North America, 4, 19, 25, 30–31, 32, 33, 35, 39, 40, 45, 54, 56, 57, 58, 61, 62, 65, 66
nothosaur, 29
Oligocene epoch, 14, 56–58
oviraptor, 36
Pacific Ocean, 31, 66
Palo Alto, California, 31
Pangaea, 20, 21, 26, 27, 29, 31, 32
Permian period, 14, 20, 26–27, 50, 52
Petrified Forest National Park, 28
placodont, 29
Playfair, John, 12
Pleistocene Ice Age, 55, 59, 61
plesiosaur, 41
Precambrian time, 14, 15
pre-Clovis theory, 62–66
pterodactyl, 41, 42
pterosaur, 29, 42
reptile, 4, 26, 27, 29, 33–52, 53, 58

rocks
    gneisses, 17
    granite, 10, 11, 17
    greenstone, 17
    igneous, 11, 17
    komatiite, 17, 18
    limestone, 10, 11, 31
    metamorphic, 17
    quartz, 31, 70
    sandstone, 11, 12
    schistus, 12
    sedimentary, 10–11, 13, 17
    shale, 10, 11, 31
sauropod, 43, 46
sauroposeidon, 44
seismosaurus, 44
Siberia, 20, 61, 62, 63, 64, 65, 66
Siccar Point, Scotland, 12
Smith, William, 12
South America, 4, 19, 21, 32, 62, 63, 65
Spirit Caveman, 63–64
stegosaurus, 42, 43
supersaurus, 44
Tethys Sea, 19, 32, 54
thecodont, 29
therapsid, 26, 29, 42
theropod, 36, 45
Triassic period, 14, 27, 28, 29
triceratops, 36, 46, 48
troodon, 36–37
tyrannosaurus (T-Rex), 4, 37, 38, 47–48
ultrasaurus, 44
velociraptor, 44
Wegener, Alfred, 21
Witwatersrand, South Africa, 17–18